A Mezuzah
on the Door

To my mother, who taught me to love books, cherish Judaism, and revere the laws of grammar.
—A.M.

To Bruce and Cisco, who make my house a home because they are in it.
—J.F.

KAR-BEN PUBLISHING, INC.
A division of Lerner Publishing Group
241 First Avenue North
Minneapolis, MN 55401 U.S.A.
1-800-4KARBEN

Website address: www.karben.com

Library of Congress Cataloging-in-Publication Data

Meltzer, Amy, 1968–
    A mezuzah on the door / by Amy Meltzer ; illustrated by Janice Fried.
        p. cm.
    Summary: Noah has not had a good night's sleep since moving from a noisy apartment in the city to a quiet house in the suburbs, but that changes after his parents invite former neighbors to celebrate the dedication of their new house as a Jewish home.
    ISBN-13: 978–1–58013–249–7 (lib. bdg. : alk. paper)
    ISBN-10: 1–58013–249–9 (lib. bdg. : alk. paper)
    [1. Moving, Household—Fiction. 2. Jews—Fiction. 3. Neighbors—Fiction. 4. Mezuzah—Fiction. 5. Judaism—Customs and practices—Fiction.] I. Fried, Janice, ill. II. Title.
PZ7.M51646Mez 2007
[E]—dc22   2006027545

Manufactured in the United States of America
1 2 3 4 5 6 – JR – 12 11 10 09 08 07

A Mezuzah
on the Door

by Amy Meltzer

illustrated by Janice Fried

KAR-BEN
PUBLISHING

It had been a month since Noah's family moved from an apartment in the city to a house in the suburbs.

"You'll love it!" his mom and dad had promised. "There will be much more space and a lot less noise."

Noah agreed. There was more space, and there was less noise.

achoo *achoo* *achoo*

But since they moved he'd had trouble sleeping. He missed the sounds he used to hear through the walls.

He remembered the clank and clunk he heard when Mrs. Feldman washed the dinner dishes. It seemed as if she always broke a glass or plate. Then there were the loud *achoos* when Mr. Gollis sneezed – always in threes. "I'm allergic to cats," he would explain. (Mr. Gollis didn't have a cat!)

Noah even missed Maya's violin practice. She seemed to have been working on *Twinkle, Twinkle Little Star* for as long as he could remember.

Noah tossed and turned, and
tossed and turned. It seemed like
hours before he finally fell asleep.

"Good morning!" said Noah's mother
cheerfully when he came down to
breakfast. "How did you sleep?"

"Not so great," said Noah. "It's too
quiet in this house."

"I'm sorry, honey. But I hope you're not too tired to celebrate, because tonight is our *Hanukkat Habayit*."

"Hanukkah? But Mom, it's only August! Hanukkah isn't until winter!"

"Not Hanukkah, Noah," his mother laughed. "Hanukkat Habayit. It's a party to celebrate our new home. 'Hanukkah' means to dedicate. We'll dedicate our home as a Jewish home, just like the Maccabees dedicated the Holy Temple."

"I remember," Noah said. "After they got rid of all the Greek idols, they cleaned the Temple and then lit the menorah."

"Exactly! The Maccabees were celebrating that the Temple was a Jewish space again."

"So we're inviting people to come clean our house? That doesn't sound like much fun!" exclaimed Noah.

"No, of course not," replied his mother. "We dedicate our home by placing a mezuzah on the doorpost. This morning we're going to the gift shop at the synagogue and you can pick a mezuzah for your room, too."

In the car Noah's mom said, "You haven't been sleeping well since we moved. What's bothering you?"

"I don't know, Mom," Noah replied. "The new house is so quiet. I feel sort of lonely in my bedroom. It's funny, but I miss hearing Maya play her violin and Mrs. Feldman dropping dishes."

"And Mr. Gollis sneezing." chimed in his mother.

"It's his allergies!" they said together and giggled as they pulled into the parking lot.

The gift shop had dozens of different mezuzah cases made of clay, glass, metal, and even olive wood from Israel.

Noah peered over the glass case. "I like this one." He pointed to a shiny blue mezuzah with a clear window at the top. "You can see tiny Hebrew letters on the paper inside."

"That's parchment." smiled the man behind the counter. "It's called a *klaf*. It's made from the skin of a kosher animal."

"Like the Torah?" asked Noah.

"Yes. It's actually a lot like the Torah. Both the Torah and the mezuzah are handwritten in Hebrew by a *sofer*, a scribe. And the words of the *Shema*, which are written in the mezuzah, come from the Torah."

"Wow," said Noah.

That night, the doorbell chimed
often as the guests arrived.
    "*Mazel Tov*," said Mr. Zundel,
Maya's father. "Your new
home is beautiful."

    "But who would
want to clean so
many rooms?" Mrs.
Feldman whispered to her husband.
    "Is there a cat here?" sneezed Mr.Gollis.

After everyone had arrived, Noah's father called the guests to gather at the front door.

"We're so glad that you could come to our Hanukkat Habayit to help us dedicate our new home as a Jewish home," he began. Then he carefully put a klaf into a beautiful silver mezuzah case.

He placed the mezuzah on the doorpost, and hammered nails at the top and bottom. When he was finished, Noah's parents recited a blessing together, and everyone answered, "Amen!"

As they came back into the house, many of the guests touched the mezuzah, and some kissed their fingertips.

"What are they doing, Mom?" Noah asked.

"People have different reasons for touching the mezuzah when they enter and leave a home," she answered. "Some people do it to remind them of the *mitzvot*, God's commandments. Others do it because they think of the mezuzah as a sign of God's protection. And some people do it because it is a custom in their families. They have seen their parents and grandparents do it. When I touch a mezuzah, I feel like I'm holding hands with everyone else who has touched it."

"Come, Noah," his father called. "Let's put your mezuzah up." The guests moved on to Noah's bedroom. His mother nailed the mezuzah to the doorpost, low enough for Noah to reach it. Some of Noah's friends and family touched his mezuzah as they left the room.

"Who's hungry?" Noah's mother asked.
The once quiet house grew noisy as the guests
sampled delicious cakes and cookies, shared stories,
and complimented Noah's family on their new home.

Maya, who had brought her violin along for the occasion, began an enthusiastic rendition of *Twinkle, Twinkle, Little Star.*

When everyone was finished celebrating, Mrs. Feldman turned to Noah's mother. "It was lovely of you to invite us. I insist on helping with the dishes." And before Noah's mother could stop her, Mrs. Feldman had put a stack of dessert plates into a sink full of soapy water. There was a clank, then a clunk, and then a loud, "Whoops! Sorry about that!" as a dish crashed to the floor.

Mr. Gollis was suddenly overcome with sneezes. "Oh, these horrible - *achoo!* - allergies - *achoo!* Are you sure there is no - *achoo!* - cat here?"

Sneezing, fiddling, clapping, clanking, clunking...so much noise! But soon the guests left and the house was quiet again.

Noah went up to his room to put on his pajamas. "We'll come up to kiss you goodnight in a few minutes," his parents said.

Noah stood at his door and looked up at his new mezuzah. He paused for a moment. Then he put his fingertips on the blue case. He thought about all of his friends and family who had touched and kissed it. And suddenly he didn't feel so lonely.

By the time Noah's mother and father came up to kiss him goodnight, Noah was fast asleep.

And for the first time since moving to his
new house, Noah had a good night's sleep.

About the Mezuzah

Mezuzah means "doorpost," and the word is often used to describe the decorative case placed on the doorpost of a Jewish home. However, the term correctly refers to the *klaf*, the small parchment scroll that is placed inside the case. The klaf, which must be handwritten in Hebrew by a scribe, contains two passages from the Biblical book of Deuteronomy (Chapter 6, verses 4-9 and Chapter 11, verses 13-21). They affirm the belief in One God who commands us to follow the commandments and to affix a mezuzah to the doorpost as a reminder.

The mezuzah should be placed in the top third of the right side of a door, tilted to face inward. Most Jewish families place a mezuzah on the front door of their homes; others put them on the doors of every room excluding the bathrooms.

The following prayer is recited when placing a mezuzah on a door:

בָּרוּךְ אַתָּה יְיָ אֱלֹהֵינוּ מֶלֶךְ הָעוֹלָם
אֲשֶׁר קִדְּשָׁנוּ בְּמִצְוֹתָיו וְצִוָּנוּ לִקְבּוֹעַ מְזוּזָה.

Baruch Atah Adonai Eloheinu melech ha'olam
Asher kid'shanu b'mitzvotav v'tzivanu likboa mezuzah.

Blessed are You, Adonai
Who has commanded us to affix the mezuzah.